EX-BOYFRIEND'S COCKY DILF

Straight to Gay First Time MM

Michael Levi

CONTENTS

CHAPTER 1

It should be a beautiful night, but how was it going to be so when my mind kept going back to what my friend had told me when I was talking to him over the phone.

He was having an affair with another man! I just couldn't wrap my mind around it. He never told me he was bisexual, so I kept on wondering what was up with that.

I took a deep breath after remembering that I just broke up with my boyfriend. I knew that his father had to be furious about it. He was just so happy that we were together, and now this happened.

At least I was in my bedroom in the college's dormitory, so I didn't have to worry about anything or anyone bothering me right now. I was bored, though.

I kept on thinking about how I would be feeling right now if I had a date with someone. After breaking up with my boyfriend, I didn't know if I was ready for another relationship, though. Maybe I'd never be.

Either way, that hardly mattered right now. What mattered was finding something to help me pass the time. I had a cat and he wasn't around as usual. Where was he? I didn't know. He had to have gone out again to play with his other cat friends.

I sighed again, rolling over on my stomach in the bed before reaching out with my hand and grabbing my phone. What should I do right now? Should I load up one of my games and play it? I had no idea.

I didn't feel like doing that at all. I wasn't just bored, after all. I was horny. *So fucking horny right now.* I could fuck anything and anyone tonight, and it was a pity that I couldn't.

I jumped out of bed and then rushed over to the bathroom. I stood in front of the mirror and checked myself out. I took a couple pictures using my phone and then I uploaded them to Tinder. What was I thinking I was doing with those pictures? The answer was pretty obvious. I was going out on the hunt. I was going to find someone to date tonight.

It didn't have to be the right person or anything of the sort. It only had to be someone fuckable. Nothing more than that. My dick was so hard right now I felt it was even bigger than normal, which was not normal, I thought as I chuckled.

I headed back to the bedroom and then fell onto the bed, my hands holding my phone in front of my face. I was shortsighted and since I didn't want to be using my glasses right now, this was about the only thing I could do here.

After uploading the photos, I checked who was available in the area. There were some guys and they were hot, but they weren't anyone worth the effort. At least, that was what I was thinking while I masturbated. My pants were lowered and my cock and my balls were free and so hot right now.

If anyone were to open the door, they would find me half naked on my bed. Certainly not a good sight that would be, of course.

Even though those guys were hot, they weren't exactly my type when it came to making me cum. They just weren't worth the effort. Not to mention that whenever I initiated a conversation with them, it never went anywhere or they always stopped texting me.

Things were certainly not looking up.

I took a deep breath again and then I rolled over on the mattress, and just when I figured I was only wasting my time, being so horny while crying as I thought about my boyfriend over and over again, a notification popped up on the screen of my phone.

The first thing that crossed my mind was that I had to be imagining things. For starters, when I selected the age range on the app, I specifically said that I didn't want to see anyone over the age of 30. Since I was only 20, it would be weird to date anyone who was already 30 years old. Although, I had to admit that some 30-year-olds looked better than their age. Some even looked young enough to be confused as being 20-year-olds.

But enough was enough about all that. Since that guy wanted to talk to me, then this was exactly what I was going to do. So, I pressed my finger on the notification and read his message.

Was I really going to date an older man? It certainly felt that that was exactly what was going to happen. Maybe I was feeling more adventurous right now, but if that was truly the case or not, I had no idea. There was something about him that was stirring something deep in me, and that was making my cock harder than it already was.

Gosh, if this kept up, I would have to relieve myself in the bathroom before even meeting up with the guy. Even though I had a lot of energy in me, it wouldn't be enough for another round with the guy, so most of all, at the moment, I just didn't want to disappoint him.

He didn't have a face, so I knew that I was taking a risk by talking to him.

He did appear to be interested in continuing this, though.

Prof123: should we meet up tonight? You can come to my house. I live alone, so you don't need to worry about anyone finding out about this.

Me: sure thing. Why not? I'm so bored right now I might as well go and meet up with you.

I sent him a dick pic, which he loved. The emoji on the screen showed me as much. I hoped that my cock was nice enough for him. He couldn't judge the size, and he wouldn't, anyway. Even though, when it came to gay sex, guys like him enjoyed experimenting with their submissive partners, I didn't think something like that was going to happen tonight. He was going to be the dominating one, of course. He was older than me and given the photos of his body, he was fit and worked out often, not to mention that he also probably took supplements and followed the right diet and everything else.

There was something about his body, though that appeared to be familiar to me and I couldn't quite put my finger on it.

Whatever that was, it wasn't going to change anything. So, I headed to his home and... I then soon realized the path I was following was more familiar than I'd thought possible.

Shit. This couldn't really be happening.

CHAPTER 2

But it was and there wasn't anything I could do about it. There wasn't anything I could do about it because my pickup truck was already positioned just outside his house and he was already looking out the window and at me.

He wore a plain white shirt, jeans pants, and white socks. Even though I was still inside my pickup truck, I could smell the perfume he sprayed on his body. It was intense and intoxicating. It made me have thoughts about him I should have buried a long time ago.

He was none other than my boyfriend's father, and I just couldn't wrap my head around it. So, he was the one on Tinder? What did he think he was doing, dating someone so much younger than him?

I didn't know, but at this point, there was no point in continuing to be in my pickup truck anymore. So, I headed out after turning off the engine and closing the door. I wasn't going to deny that it was weird, thinking about him being my boyfriend's old man while I wanted to fuck him so bad right now.

No more than a few seconds later, I was outside the door of his house. It really was the same house I had been to so many times before breaking up with Dean.

This was going to be tough, no matter how I tried to maneuver through it.

Frederick opened the door and let me inside the house. "I never thought that you were the one on Tinder."

"You don't really find it odd that you are trying to date me even though I was Dean's boyfriend?"

He put his arm on the wall by our side, leaning his body against it. "Are you really worried about that? Does it turn you off?" He asked. I had always thought that he was such a huge turn-on, but I never thought that we would be on the verge of dating and fucking.

"I mean, I suppose it doesn't really matter as long as Dean doesn't find out anything about this."

"He doesn't have to find out anything about what you're going to do, as long as you are okay with it."

There was a moment of silence. We were still both looking at each other's eyes and there was so much being said this way. He wanted me. His eyes continued to go up and down slowly as he examined my body in its entirety.

"You're beautiful."

"And you are hot as fuck, and also pretty cocky."

His smirk widened. It wasn't the first time I noticed how cocky he looked. Frederick was always cocky and I knew that would never change about him.

His muscles were like they were sculpted. The shadows formed perfectly around his body. His shirt was tight, but not too much so, clinging around his body as though it didn't want to leave. Sweat drops formed on his forehead and chest, making me want to be running my tongue all over his skin.

Oh, and did I say anything about the height difference? He was so much taller than me that it wasn't even a contest. Even though he was older than me and, in most cases, the younger man was taller, it wasn't the case at all here. Not only that, I was puny in comparison to his much bigger, manlier body.

I gulped. What else was I going to do right now when I was inside his house and he could do whatever he wanted to do to me?

"Are you sure that nobody is going to come? I thought you were married. You told me that you live alone, but I don't think that's exactly true."

"Don't worry about my wife. She's not going to come. Not

anymore, anyway."

"You broke up with her?" I asked, sounding breathless. How else was I going to be sounding when it never occurred to me that they had problems in their marriage?

"Yeah, something like that. I was just fed up with her, so I was the one that decided to break up with her. I kicked her out of my house. That's what happened."

After saying that, he leaned off the wall and then proceeded to me. His footsteps were slow but weighted. He knew what he was doing. Frederick knew the impact that he was having on me.

I couldn't help but steal glances at his bulge. Even though he wore jeans, it was like it was growing bigger as the seconds continued to pass. So, what the hell was I even thinking I was going to do from this moment onwards? That I was going to fall down to my knees and I was going to suck him off?

Ridiculous.

I would never do that without feeling so ashamed of myself.

Still, he was pressing on and now he was nearer to me than he had ever been. I could smell the perfume coming from his body stronger than ever before, and it made my dick give somersaults under my pants.

"It doesn't really strike you as odd that you are going to have sex with me?" I asked, but it was obvious that Frederick didn't really give a damn about that. So much so that he planted his hands on my cheeks and then kissed me without warning.

And even though I should be furious about this, the fact was that I welcomed it. His lips were unbelievably soft.

CHAPTER 3

He pulled his head back at about that same moment and some seconds after connecting his lips to mine. I could even hear his heavy breathing. Or maybe that was just my breathing getting heavier over time and only now I was hearing it.

"Did you like that?" He asked, putting his fingers under my shirt and then beginning to lift it up. His eyes were locked with mine and I knew that he was only going to proceed from this moment onward with my permission.

At least for that, he needed it.

My throat was dry. What was I supposed to say? He wasn't exactly taking advantage of me. I was welcoming this as much as pretty much everything that ever happened in my life, and he also knew that I was gay. I just never thought that he was into men as well.

"Yeah, it was pretty nice."

"Do you want a little bit more than that?"

"Aren't you going to answer my previous question?" I insisted. Even though my cock was hard and everything in my body was begging for me to have sex with Frederick, it was so difficult for me to take the next step. Every time that I thought about it, memories of me and my boyfriend rushed back into my mind.

"About Dean? Oh, come on. You can't be really serious about that. I know what you want. I know how hard you are right now and how your asshole is clenching and unclenching because of me. You want me deep inside of you, isn't that right?" He murmured, putting his hands on my shoulders and then leading me inside the bedroom.

This was actually Dean's bedroom. I came here so many times. I didn't really stay in touch with him anymore, so I didn't really know what he was doing at the moment. I supposed that he was probably studying for the Marine Biology midterms.

That being the case, it meant I had all the time in the world to do whatever I wanted with Frederick. And he was so hot right now and so into this. So much so that he was, before long, kissing me one more time.

His eyes locked with me and even though I didn't want to do this, my hand went down and I found his bulge. I began to massage it tentatively as though I was giving all the signs that we were going to go on with this. It was plump and big, and I could also feel the outline of his cock through the pants.

"That's exactly what I was fearing was going to happen when I came here."

"I think you just need to grow up a little more. I can help you with that. There is no shame in having sex with me. After all, you can think of me as just being another guy. I'm older than you, and that's something I can never erase, but it only adds to the spice behind this moment, don't you think?" He murmured into my ear.

I nodded as I gave him the information he needed. My mouth was watering as I wondered more and more about how his cock looked when it was out of his pants. I knew he was imagining the same, though concerning my shaft. It was throbbing and so stiff right now I just wanted to masturbate. It was such a pity that I couldn't do so without giving Frederick everything he wanted.

"That's exactly what I've been thinking. I want you so much. Even though it might be something you think is coming out of nowhere right now, the truth is that I have always wanted to do this. Even when you were still with Dean, I was still thinking about you so much," he murmured before lifting my shirt and taking it off my body.

I didn't work out. Even though my body was lean, there was nothing special about it. My physique was small compared to his, and it couldn't really be any different. It only added to the fact that he was the dominant one in our sex.

He ran his fingers along my body and then he got down on his knees in front of me. It was quite weird to see such a massive man on his knees before me, but I wasn't going to complain. Pre-come was oozing out from the tip of my gland, and we could both already smell the scent in the air.

"Gosh, you are so beautiful," he murmured more to himself than to me. He lowered my pants and then my pair of boxer briefs. My cock jumped out looking proud and begging for Frederick's attention.

He grabbed it as soon as he had access to it, running his fingers on it. I was cut. His eyes could see the veins snaking along my shaft. My balls were aching and hung low. They were filled with milk. After my break up with Dean, I didn't masturbate, still thinking about him and how good his shaft felt inside of me. It was a pity that we would never do it again, though I wasn't going to complain I was having sex with Frederick.

There was something incredibly wrong about this, but it was the taboo factor behind it that made me crave this moment as much as I was. Pre-come continued to ooze out from the gland of my shaft and he ran his fingers over it, coating them.

After licking his fingers one after the other, Frederick smiled, and then he stood up. He pressed his hands on my shoulders and then brought me against the wall behind me. His eyes locked with me one more time before he kissed me again. This time, he was much braver about what he was doing. He smashed his body against mine and I even felt his junk pressing against my belly.

I moaned and groaned as his hands continued to explore my torso.

I was beyond being saved right now. I wanted Frederick so much at this point, so much so that my hand was already going down and looking for his gargantuan shaft.

CHAPTER 4

"I knew you were going to do this," he murmured into my mouth before kissing me. I felt the salty taste of my pre-come on my lips. I should be disgusted by it, but I felt exactly the opposite.

"Do you like it?" He murmured, running his finger on my lips.

"I never thought I would say this, but I think I love it. I want more."

He smiled, coating his finger with more of my pre-come. I was just so hard right now that more of it continued to ooze out. After lowering his body, he stood up again and then he neared his fingers to my lips, letting me run my tongue over them.

The salty taste was incredible, I thought as I closed my eyes and basked in it.

After that was done, Frederick got back down on his knees and then he closed his eyes before encapsulating my gland in his mouth. I never thought he was going to do that. Such an imposing man and he was putting himself in such a submissive position to me. I didn't even know what was going on in his head.

But he was still enjoying it, I realized as he continued to drive and run his tongue over my gland. It was incredibly sensitive, and I felt my orgasm coming up. It wasn't going to be long from now until I was shooting it out inside his mouth. Was that really his plan? I didn't know, but I couldn't even think about it much.

Not satisfied with this, Frederick cupped my balls and began to play with them. His fingers showed his experience as he got me so much closer to my climax. I closed my eyes before realizing how heavy my breathing had become. Sweat pooled on my forehead and in my armpits.

We didn't even start this properly yet and things were already getting out of control.

Of course, before coming here, I'd shaven my balls, something I was sure Frederick appreciated a lot, given how hungry his fingers were while playing and fumbling with my nuts right now.

But just when I thought that he was going to go all the way with this, he took my shaft out of his mouth. To say that I was puzzled would be an understatement. What was going on in his mind right now?

"Why?" I asked, my whole body still resonating with the pleasure overflowing from it.

"It's not going to be so easy. At least, I don't want to make you come right now."

"You want to drag this for a lot longer than it needs to happen, right?" I asked, noticing his intentions.

"That and a lot more, William," he murmured as he replied to me. I knew that he was cocky and an asshole, but I didn't think that he was so much those things. He kept lowering and raising his hand along my dick, pushing the skin up and down. Even though he took my shaft out of my mouth, he was still doing everything in his power to keep me in a state where my climax was on the verge of happening.

I missed the warmth and the wetness of his mouth. My dick was so slick right now too, and the gland was rosy. Pre-come just couldn't stop seeping out.

"What are you going to do now?" I asked when I realized that his teasing was only going to continue and I couldn't do anything about it.

"Something we should do so that you are prepared for when I penetrate you," he said before standing up.

So, just like that, the orgasm that I was feeling in my body was dissipating. Again, Frederick was an asshole and there was nothing in the world that could change that.

He took me to the other side of the bedroom, from where he

picked up something. It was a dildo. It looked just like a dick. I never thought that Dean had one. He never told me anything about it, and now it looked like Frederick was going to fuck me with it.

"Get on the bed and open your ass. I'm going to see if you can take it. If you can, then it means that I can fuck you without having to worry about anything. I don't like to brag, but my shaft is so much bigger than this."

The dildo he was holding was easily 9 inches long and who knew how many inches thick. And that was me being conservative with my estimates.

Well, there was no point in wasting any time, so I did exactly what he asked of me. I lied down on the bed and opened my ass for him. He walked until he was standing behind me, and then he positioned himself on top of me. No more than a few seconds later, he pressed the tip of the dildo into my anus, and I arched my back in response.

It wasn't even properly inside of me yet, and I already felt so much pain flaring in my body.

"You are so tight and your asshole is so pinky," he murmured behind me before running his finger in my ass crack. After doing that, he pressed the dildo slightly further inside of me. I felt as though I was taking the biggest dump in all of my life, and that was putting it mildly.

I knew that, after this, walking would be so difficult, but I was still welcoming it.

CHAPTER 5

"Oh fuck, oh fuck," I hissed as I grabbed the pillow in front of me and clutched it to my face. I began to scream into it. It was the only thing I could do right now to deal with some of the pain I was feeling. It was overwhelming.

Some seconds after that, when Frederick realized that he was almost killing me with the pain he was inflicting on me, he stopped moving the dildo deeper inside of me.

"Are you okay?" He asked after noticing the tears running down my cheeks. I never thought that I would feel so much pain in my asshole. Every time that Dean fucked me before, it wasn't like this at all.

"Yeah, I'm okay." I took a deep breath, trying to dry my tears on the pillow. "It's just that the dildo is so much bigger than Dean's cock."

He chuckled. "That's disappointing, considering that he came from me."

I didn't say anything about that, rolling my eyes inside my head. I never thought that he would point out something so... Inappropriate and which made him seem so much cockier than he already looked initially.

"Can we please actually stop talking about Dean?" I begged. It was the only thing I could do so that this moment felt less weird.

"Sure. It's like he doesn't really exist, or at least I'm going to try to make it so," he murmured as he ran his hand over my thigh. It was so big it made my thigh feel smaller than it was. Again, I didn't have strong muscles and my body wasn't big at all, but I was still no pushover.

After doing that, he pushed the dildo a little further inside of me and I screamed into the pillow as much as I could. It was stifled by the material, and I was so happy it was. I was pretty sure that some of the neighbors remembered me, so when they realized that I came here and if they heard screams coming from inside the house, they would tell everyone about them.

"Almost fully in there," he murmured behind me before sliding the dildo further inside of me. Even though it was dazzlingly long, it was the thickness that made me feel as though I was going to black out.

No more than some seconds later, Frederick finally announced, "there. It's all the way inside of you, and I bet you are loving this. Now I begin to realize why Dean fell in love with you and why he broke up with you. You are a slut, and there is no denying that."

I turned my head to look at him. I never thought he would say something so inappropriate, which was even more so than the thing about him being bigger than Dean.

He smirked before starting to move the dildo forward and backward in my rectum. Pain flared up in my body again, and now it was slightly less than before, but it was still as capable of making me black out.

A couple of seconds later, he stopped after realizing that I wasn't screaming as loudly as I was before. I was still moaning and groaning loudly. I felt so much pleasure that my dick was incredibly hard right now, and I was using this opportunity, with my body lying on the mattress, to grind it on it. I was on the verge of coming, and this time, differently from when I came here, nothing was going to stop me from doing that.

Or even someone else. Although, just when I thought I was going to climax over the bedsheets, he slapped my butt without showing any mercy. It was a strong slap that reverberated in the bedroom. I arched my back and my body flinched. I never thought that someone could slap me with so much strength. It even left a welt on my skin.

"Again, I'm not going to let you come so soon."

I rolled over on my back, my hands going to my dick. I began to pump it vigorously. I closed my eyes and felt how close I was to reaching my climax. I could even feel that pressure sensation close to the head of my cock.

However, just when I realized that I could really do this and that this time Frederick wouldn't be able to stop me, I realized how silly I was being right now. So, I opened my eyes the moment he began to undress.

Oh my God. His body was even bigger and more perfect than I thought. He was literally made of muscles. The definition was nothing short of mouthwatering. The shadows formed and danced around his muscles, the highlights standing out so much. And it was all heightened by the fact that there was a layer of wetness on his skin.

Even though the lighting in the bedroom wasn't favorable, his skin seemed so lust-inducing. It made me want to be with my hands sliding all over his curves, something I was sure he was thinking about as well.

"Do you really want to waste the best moment of our night?" He asked before putting his fingers around his shaft and pumping it. The way that he was doing that was frenetic from the get-go, and the best part about that was that he was aiming it right at me.

He was going to shoot his come all over me, and that realization sent shivers of pleasure all through my body. I just never thought it would happen, and much less when I was still lying on my boyfriend's bed.

My eyes went wide. I barely had enough time to process what was going on when ropes of come began to shoot out from the tip of his dick. They coated me and made my skin feel sticky, and it was the best sensation in my life in a very long time.

I would never forget it.

CHAPTER 6

Things were far from over between us, though. I actually woke up the next morning with my head feeling heavy. I opened my eyes and I found a tray with breakfast on it. I dug in right away without even thinking about why this was happening. The food was tasty and it smelled nice. How could I think that anything was wrong with this?

And truly, nothing was wrong with anything. Just when I was asking myself where Frederick was, he appeared in the doorway. I must have blacked out yesternight after he came all over me and shot his load over my begging skin. I would never forget that.

I glanced down when I realized he was holding something in his right hand. I blinked twice in a row to process what it was. It was a butt plug. Whoa. I didn't think we were already going to be moving to the next step in our date, which was still going on.

"I know that you just woke up and that you've just finished eating your breakfast, but I think it's about time I did this," he announced before coming over to me slowly and carefully.

Frederick waited for me to roll over on my stomach and I did that some seconds later. He put the tray with the devoured breakfast away and then he reached inside the nightstand. From there, he grabbed a bottle of lube, which he screwed open in an instant. After doing that, he spread the liquid on his hand. After his fingers were coated with the substance, he started to smear my butthole with it.

The way his fingers were moving and turning inside my

rectum made me feel as though I was going to climax. It was such a pity that I was unable to do that when he was shooting his load all over me last night. It would have been a tremendous moment for that.

I wasn't going to complain about it, though.

Seconds later, when he realized that my asshole was completely coated with the oily substance, he began to force the butt plug inside it. I felt pain just like I thought I was going to, but it was still not as much as when he fucked me with the dildo. That was a memory I would never forget.

"How are you feeling? Still feeling guilty about this? Still thinking about Dean?" He asked while running his hand on my backside. His fingers were decisive and he knew exactly what he was doing. I basked in the warmth coming from his fingers, and I soon found myself hard again.

After remembering that he came all over me yesternight and that I didn't yet have time to take a shower, I noticed that the smell of come was still intense in the air.

Nothing I could do about that, though. But I had to admit to myself I quite liked it and wouldn't have this happen any other way.

Some seconds after that, he inserted the butt plug all the way inside of my tunnel, and it felt full, although not as full as it did yesternight. Even though I couldn't turn my head and look over my shoulder, I knew that Frederick was delighted by what his eyes were witnessing.

"There," he said before giving my butt a slap that, again, reverberated in the bedroom. "You can turn back around."

I did that right away.

I stood up after getting out of bed and then I turned around so that I could check my behind in the mirror. After yesternight, I was still completely naked, so I could see my back and everything else without difficulty. I just realized that there was something different with the butt plug. After shaking my hips, it flashed.

So that meant that every time I walked around, the butt plug would flash and make me feel uncomfortable. That also meant

I couldn't get out of his house until he had his way with me. Interesting.

"Do you like it?" He asked without showing any shame in his voice. He was hard right now, especially after seeing me naked with the butt plug flashing.

I smiled. How was I going to say no to something like that?

"You are punishing me?"

"No. I'm not quite doing that. I'm not really punishing you. I'm only doing this so that you understand that I have full control over you now."

After a moment of silence, I asked, "so, when are you finally going to take the virginity of my ass?"

"Hmm, should I really do that today? I don't think so. I think that I want to wait until the moment is right. Again, I don't want to see you blacking out like how it happened last night. It was terrible," he lamented while shaking his head in shame.

It was as though he regretted it, which couldn't be further from the truth.

"I'm going to lounge by the swimming pool right now. I feel like relaxing a little after that spicy night we had. Don't you feel the same way? Don't you want to come with me?" He asked, his fingers enclosing his dick and then stroking it. I knew what was going on in his mind right now and why he was doing this. He was teasing me.

"That's exactly what I want to do," I replied after going outside with him. After doing that, he lied on the lounge chair by the swimming pool, keeping his legs spread out apart and his dick on full display. Thanks to the walls around the property, we didn't have to worry about people snooping on us.

I couldn't believe that I was being so submissive without saying anything about it.

"Suck me off," he demanded, which was the only command he needed to give me right now, and I obeyed without saying anything about it.

I took his dick inside my mouth for the first time and it was the best thing ever... until the moment when he finally took the virginity of my ass, that was.

CHAPTER 7

I was sleeping when I realized he brought some people with him. I barely had enough time to process who they were before noticing that it wasn't going to be so easy. They were all hung as fuck. They had just entered the room where I was, and were marching toward me after noticing that the look in my eyes told them that they could do whatever they wanted to me right now. After all, my body was begging for it.

"Sorry for the sudden intrusion, but we just couldn't wait anymore for this moment. It's been days, hasn't it?" Frederick asked while approaching me. He was already hard and his dick was pointing at me. It was like he could read exactly what was going on in my mind, just how much I was thinking about rubbing my lips around his massive, oversized shaft. And after that happened, who knew what else I would do.

He was talking about my butt plug. Of course, he couldn't be talking about anything else. It had been in my rectum for days already, and even though I still felt it, it was like it had become a part of me.

I nodded to give him the confirmation he was looking for. It was actually a confirmation of two things. One of them was that I recognized he was right about the butt plug, and the other one was that it was also okay to proceed with this. I had no idea who his friends were, though.

Did their names even matter? I felt like this wasn't going to take long.

I turned around so that Frederick had easy access to the butt plug. He placed two of his fingers around the little loop that was at the end of the item, and then he yanked it out without measuring the strength with which he did that. After doing that, he slid and ran his hands over my body, showing me that he wanted to feel every part of me.

After the butt plug was removed, my rectum tried to close in on itself, but it couldn't. It was only missing one thing right now before Frederick and his buddies could impale me, and that was some lube.

Without saying anything else, Frederick reached over for the bottle of lube and then spread some of the substance on his fingers before he started to smear my asshole with it. His buddies were pumping their dicks slowly and carefully as they readied themselves for the final act.

So, I wasn't going to just lose the virginity of my ass, but it was also going to be a threesome. I couldn't be happier about this.

My smile couldn't fade away from my face while Frederick continued to spread the lube in my asshole. His fingers turned and moved with expertise and care. Even though I was putting myself in a position where he could be as rough to me as he wanted to, he wasn't going to do that.

After that was done, he groaned before pulling his fingers out of me. With that finished, he grabbed my thighs and then pulled me toward him with determination. I had to grimace and grit my teeth as I waited for the inevitable rounds of pain that were going to flare in my body.

"Gosh, he looks so tight," one of Frederick's buddies murmured behind me.

Just after he finished doing that, Frederick eased his prick inside of me. He waited every so often as he checked my reaction. He just wanted to make sure that I wasn't going to pass out like it happened that other time. That other time... It felt like it happened years ago.

After that, Frederick began to roll his hips as he pistoned in and out of me without showing an ounce of mercy. From the get-go, his pace was frenetic, and I could even feel his balls slapping against my butt. It was the best feeling of my life, and everything was so quiet around us that I could hear my huffs.

Seconds later, or when it felt like hours had passed, Frederick began to come inside of me. His cock throbbing and shaking, it was a feeling unlike any other while my walls clamped around it. I would never forget the experience that came with him unloading his come inside my tunnel. It was warm and incredibly sticky. It paved the way for his buddies, who were already positioning themselves behind me after he pulled out.

After that, one of them asked, "do you think that now he can take two of us at the same time?"

His other buddy replied, "yeah, I think so. Why not? You can see it on his face just how much he is enjoying every moment of this."

After saying that, he grabbed my thighs with determination, just like Frederick did, and then he impaled me without showing mercy. After that, it was much easier for me, but there was still a lot of pain. I arched my back as I realized just how difficult breathing was becoming right now.

No more than some minutes after that, they both came inside of me after they eased their pricks to the hilt. I came as well as I shot my milk on the bed sheets, and after all of that was over, I closed my eyes and I really thought I was going to pass out, but I didn't.

I didn't because this was far from over. Even though these were guys over 30 years old, they still had more milk to share with me. That was why they were still jerking off while pointing their shafts at me.

I couldn't erase the smile spreading on my face. I was their bitch and I loved it.

EPILOGUE

So, it had already been some days since that infamous night with Frederick and his buddies, and I still couldn't remember everything that happened. Not anymore, anyway. It was like being in this house was taking its toll on me, and even though part of me wanted to leave it, I wasn't going to.

I had a friend who knew about this, and he decided to come here to the park so that we could catch up on what we missed between us after we both went to different colleges.

My body was hunched over and my arms were on my legs while I interlaced my fingers. My eyes scanned the surrounding environment, the trees, the people perambulating, and some squirrels hiding in the trees.

I felt a hand settling on my shoulder when I flung my head to where it came from. It took me a while to realize this, but he was just my buddy. He was gay just like I was. After I told him that I'd decided to become Frederick's boyfriend, he wanted to meet up with me.

He came here from another state. His hand was holding a smoothie, and he gave me the second one he was holding in his left hand. The taste was strawberry with chocolate, and it spread over my tongue like something made by the gods. It was getting hot around this time of the summer season, and so the smoothie came at just about the right time.

"Hey, I heard about what you were doing. I didn't think that you were just going to dump Dean," he lamented while trying to make this look less weird than it was. But it wasn't working. I said that I would even marry Dean, but that was now in the past.

"I'm not really thinking about that. I'm just happy that you are here and spending some time with me. There's so much we need to talk about," I confessed, putting the straw in my mouth and sucking on it. The smoothie flowed into my mouth and graced my tongue with its sweet taste.

"I know."

"What are you going to do now that you know that it looks like things are going well for you in your life?" I asked, curious about that.

Jason looked up after sucking from the smoothie's straw again. The white clouds were moving slowly and shyly in the clear, blue sky. It was such a beautiful sight that it made me wonder if our relationship would ever last for all of eternity, just like this sky would.

"I don't really know. I'm actually thinking about something I don't even know if I should bring up or not," he murmured more to himself than to me, making me wonder what he was talking about. Was he bothered by something I was doing?

I didn't know, but I was going to poke a little bit until the truth came out.

In the meantime, I had something much more important I needed to spend my time with, and that was Frederick's dick.

After the first taste, I couldn't stop obsessing over it.

The End

Don't forget to leave your review. It really helps me a lot :)

TEASER: EX-GIRLFRIEND'S HOT DILF

Straight to Gay First Time MM (College Experiences - 4)

I didn't want anything to do with Thomas anymore after that incident with him. I still wanted to consider him my friend, but nothing more than that. That was why I moved across the country, looking for a place where I could clear up my mind.

It was working, or so I thought until a little problem showed up between me and my girlfriend. In the beginning, I thought that it was nothing, but then it grew and it turned into something that I couldn't control.

I noticed her chatting with someone on her phone. It happened so often and I could only keep on wondering what that was all about. I tried asking her about it, but she was always angry with me, so I wasn't able to poke around much until it was too late and I caught her red-handed. She was with someone else and that was something I could never forgive!

And yet, her father wanted an explanation. That was why I came here. Back to my girlfriend's house. I had to say that I didn't think I would ever come back here. My heart was tight thinking about what was going to happen now.

I sighed, lifting my hand before knocking on the door. The next thing I thought was going to happen was her coming to see me again. I heard footsteps coming from behind the door, and they were heavy and loud. Whoever was coming to the door certainly wasn't a woman.

The door opened and I found Bryan, her father. He was big. He was massive and he made me feel tiny in comparison to him. I had never felt so insignificant in front of another man. I had always thought of myself as someone who could put a hell of an effort in a fight against another man, no matter his size, but it was obvious that it would not be the case against this man.

His eyes glared at me. It was obvious that he didn't like my presence here, but since he requested it, he wasn't going to kick me away from his house… right?

Bryan was the kind of man that worked out at the local gym often, pumping weight, and he also followed an appropriate diet, and took whey protein every day after a hard workout session. He wore a flimsy, skin-tight shirt that hung around his body, highlighting his muscles.

He wasn't just bigger than me, but also taller. If I were to hug him, my arms would go under his. That was how significant the difference in size was. He could bury my head in his chest with little to no effort.

There was also this smell in the air coming from him. It appeared to be his sweat mixed with something else. It was strong, filling my nostrils. It made me have thoughts I would never have unless something different was going on with me. Something I thought would never be materializing like this.

We were just standing there, not much happening. His eyes continued to glare at me, making me wonder if he was going to kick me away from his house or invite me in.

"So, you've come," he said with gritted teeth, handing out his hand. I took it. What else would I do? I asked myself, his hand engulfing mine. So, it wasn't just his body overall that was bigger than mine, but his hand was like… I didn't even know how to properly describe it. It was like it was twice the size of my hand.

"Yeah, I did. Of course I was going to come. You wanted to see me so that we can talk a little bit about what happened between me and Heather," I explained, hoping that we were going straight to the point after this and I wouldn't have to say much more.

After all, this whole situation was just making me feel so uncomfortable.

"I'm glad that you came," he said, turning around and then I followed him inside his house. Being here for the nth time made me feel slightly weird. I didn't think that I would ever be back, especially not to be with Bryan, who was going to eat me alive with what he had to say. I couldn't imagine that it was going to be anything nice, after all.

"I'm glad, too," I said even though it was a lie. I mean, what else was I going to say?

Bryan walked in front of me, his back looking daunting and imposing. Really, it was like his back was thrice the size of mine, and me being someone that practiced football and some other sports, I liked to think that I wasn't skinny.

Either way, that was a silly notion, me comparing myself to that hunk of a man. I was always going to feel so much smaller than him.

Not to mention that his shirt also clung to his body thanks to his sweat. I knew that anybody would think that he looked hot and he did. I couldn't believe that I was admitting that right now.

"Sit," he ordered, lifting his hand and pointing to the couch that was positioned by the other side of the coffee table.

I sat down, my body feeling heavier and clumsier all of a sudden. I didn't like the direction this was taking at all.

He sat down on the other couch. I felt his weight when he did that, the seat of the couch sagging so much when he deposited his weight on it. Even now, sitting, he still looked so much bigger than anyone I knew. That man was a giant.

His biceps bulged, the veins popping out with sweat trickling down his skin. Good Lord. What the hell was he doing before he heard me knocking on the door? I asked myself, not wanting to know the answer. Was he working out? If that was the case, then I was certain he was feeling energized right now and more prone to outbursts, depending on whatever I said. I was going to have to mince my words.

I certainly didn't want to know what exactly he was thinking about me right now.

SIMILAR BOOKS

SERIES - DISCIPLINED TO SUBMISSION

1. When You're Not Looking

2. When he Comes

3. Punishing the Short Seller

SERIES - GAY FOR BLUE COLLARS

1. Given to the Cop

2. Given to the Miner

3. Given to the Plumber

4. Given to the Firefighter

5. Given to the Mechanic

ABOUT THE AUTHOR

Steamy MM stories, baby! Michael Levi can't go a day without sitting down and putting into words all the dirty scenes that sprout in his mind. His collection is diverse, but it's gay love only. And if you are looking for something free, check his mailing list. Warning: it can be extra spicy.

When Michael Levi isn't writing, he's chilling out by the lake close to his house. Nothing better than kicking back with a martini in his hand as he daydreams his next explicit scenes.

* 9 7 9 8 3 5 3 2 2 6 4 0 6 *